To Cecily.

First published in Great Britain in 2018 by Andersen Press Ltd.,
20 Vauxhall Bridge Road, London SW1V 2SA.
Copyright © David Lucas, 2018.
The rights of David Lucas to be identified as the
author and illustrator of this work have been
asserted by him in accordance with the Copyright,
Designs and Patents Act, 1988.
All rights reserved.
Printed and bound in China.
First edition.
British Library Cataloguing in Publication Data available.
ISBN 978 1 78344 605 6

I WAS MADE FOR YOU

David Lucas

Andersen Press

Cat was made from the softest, fluffiest wool.
"Why was I made?" asked Cat.

Mummy squeezed him tight and whispered,
"It's a surprise."

Cat was wrapped up with ribbon.
"Sit very still," said Mummy.
Cat sat very still. "No peeping."

Cat couldn't see out of his wrapping.
He didn't know where he was, but he
could hear laughter and a little girl singing.

"Why was I made?" asked Cat,
but nobody seemed to hear.

Then there was silence, as if the whole world were asleep.
Cat peeped out of his wrapping.

There, just in front of his nose was a label:
DaISY.
"That's not my name," said Cat. "There must be some mistake."

Cat looked out at the DaRKNeSS.
"Why was I made?" asked Cat.
He didn't expect a reply.
"Wait until morning," said the
DaRKNeSS, "then you'll see."
But Cat couldn't wait.
Cat needed answers.

Cat went to the DOOR.
"Why was I made?" asked
Cat.

"Well, I don't know about
you," said the DOOR,
swinging wide open, "but I
was made to be useful."

"I'm not sure if I'm very
useful," said Cat. And he
set off into the night.

Cat didn't notice the nasty nail or the loose thread behind him.

WHOOSH!

Cat skidded down the STEPS.
"Why was I made?" asked Cat.
"To go places," giggled the STEPS.
"But I don't know where I'm going!"
said Cat.

He fought his way through
the SNOW.
"Why was I made?" asked Cat.
"To dance!" sang the SNOW,
whirling him about.

"Um... I don't feel like dancing at the
moment," said Cat. "But thank you
anyway."

Cat climbed to the top of the ROCK.

"Why was I made?" asked Cat.

"To be strong!" boomed the ROCK.

"But I'm soft and fluffy," said Cat.

Cat spoke to the STARS.

"Why was I made?"

"To shine!" said the STARS.

"But I'm not shiny," said Cat.

The **WIND** blew Cat high in the air.
"Why was I made?" asked Cat.
"To be free!" whistled the **WIND**.
"Free?" said Cat. "Me?"

SPLASH!
Cat fell into
the **RIVER**.

The **RIVER** was icy cold.
"Blug-guggle-glug?"
asked Cat.

Cat climbed ashore, and soon
he was lost among the TREES.
"Why was I made?" asked Cat.
"To grow," whispered the TREES,
dreaming of spring.

In the morning light, Cat saw the long, loose thread trailing
away behind him, snagged on the rocks and branches.
"I'm only growing shorter," said Cat.

The **SUN** rose and its golden rays warmed the icy air.

"Why was I made?" asked Cat.

"To give," said the **SUN**.

"But what have I got to give?" said Cat.
"Yourself!" said the **SUN**.

"Give?" said Cat. "Myself?"
He was thinking hard.

"That's why I was wrapped up with ribbon
and told to sit still. I was meant as a gift!"
But who was Daisy?
And then Cat knew that, too.
"Daisy is who I'm for!"

And he pictured a little girl with no present of her own.

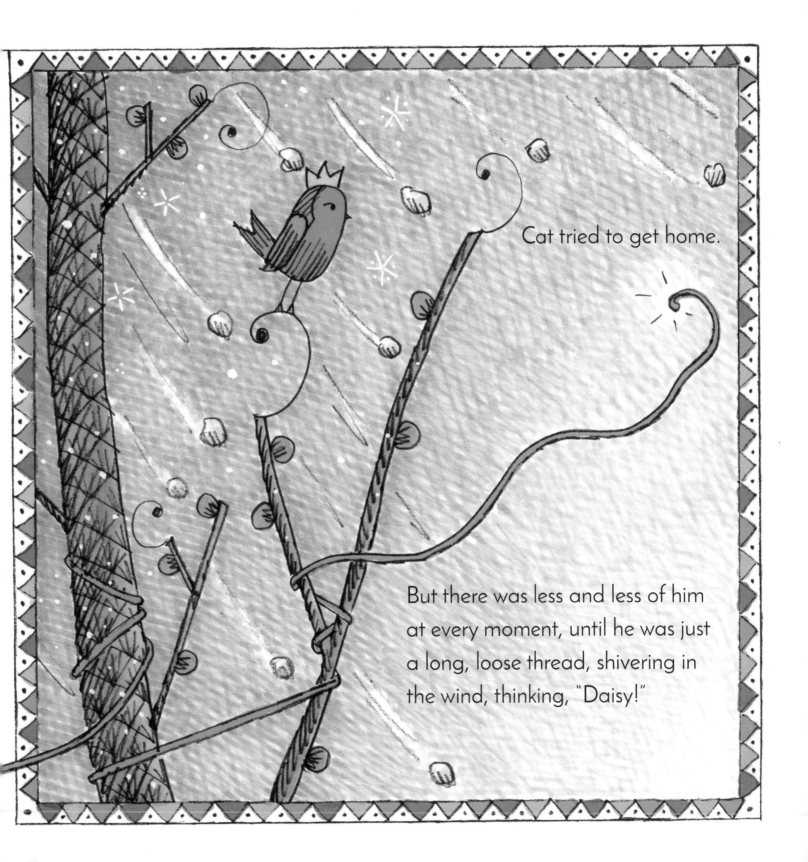

Cat tried to get home.

But there was less and less of him at every moment, until he was just a long, loose thread, shivering in the wind, thinking, "Daisy!"

On Christmas morning, Daisy had a lovely present for Mummy.

But where was Mummy's present for Daisy?

They looked for clues together. A ribbon, torn paper, a pretty label with Daisy's name.

The D O O R creaked.

"Look!" said Daisy. "A woolly thread, caught on this nasty nail."

It led them out of the DOOR,
down the STEPS and through the SNOW,
up the ROCK, along the RIVER and into the TREES.
Daisy gathered the thread and Mummy wound it into a ball.

Daisy watched as Mummy made Cat as good as new.

And then Daisy gave him a great big hug.

"I know why I was made," said Cat...

"I was made for you."